Alfie Alligator

How Big? How Tall? How Short? How Small?

Judy Hindley
Pictures by
Colin King

First published 1986 by William Collins Sons & Co Ltd, London and Glasgow
© text Judy Hindley 1986, © illustrations Colin King 1986

Tall, tall, tall –
A very tall wall.

We feel small
Near the very tall wall.

This wall is not tall.
This wall is low.

Off we all go
On the wall that is low.

Who is up high?
Who is down low?
Perhaps we should stay
On the wall that is low.

Perhaps we should climb
On the wall that is tall?
No, no!
Watch out!
It's far too high.
It's not safe to go there
Unless you can fly.

Here's my friend, Sam.

Is he short?

Is he tall?

Is he wide?

Is he thin?

Is he big?

Is he small?

He's not as tall
As the very tall wall.

He's not as tall
As the tree.

He's not as big
As a house or a tower,

But he is much taller
And bigger
Than me!

And I am much bigger
Than my friend Jane,

And Jane is much bigger
Than Fred,

Or build your nest
On a friendly moose?

Home is a hole
For a worm or a mole.

Pigs like a pen.
A coop's for a hen.

19

Some like to dwell
Inside a shell.

And fish like to swim
Where it's deep and dim.

A cat won't be pleased
If it's home for some fleas.

A mouse house is small
Behind a wall.

Frogs and crocodiles
Know where to romp.
They feel at home
In a muddy swamp.

Think about pet homes –
A cage, or a tank,

A bowl for guppies,
A box for puppies.

A plant likes soil.
That's where it grows.
And glasses are always
At home on a nose.

So castle or dolls' house,

Wigwam or dome,

Whatever it is,
There's no place like home!